SCOOTER'S TAIL OF TERROR

A FABLE OF ADDICTION AND HOPE

Written and Illustrated by Larry Shles

J

Jalmar Press
Rolling Hills Estates, California

SCOOTER'S TAIL OF TERROR
A Fable of Addiction and Hope

Library of Congess Cataloging-in-Publication Data

Shles, Larry
    Scooter's Tail of Terror: A Fable of Addiction and Hope / Written and Illustrated by Larry Shles.
          p.   cm.
    Summary: Scooter the squirrel becomes addicted to the juices, leaves, and seeds of a harmful vine and gradually loses control of his life.
    ISBN 0-915190-89-3 (pbk.) : $9.95
    [1. Drug abuse--Fiction. 2. Squirrels--Fiction.]   I. Title
    PZ7.S5585Sc   1992
    [E]--dc20
                                          92-12058
                                            CIP
                                          AC

Published by Jalmar Press

Scooter's Tail of Terror - A Fable of Addiction and Hope
Written and Illustrated: Lawrence M. Shles
Typography: Mario A. Artavia II
Project Coordinator: Jeanne Duke

Printed in the United States of America

First edition printing: 10 9 8 7 6 5 4 3 2 1

Books in the Squib Series by Larry Shles

Moths & Mothers, Feathers & Fathers

Hoots & Toots & Hairy Brutes

Hugs & Shrugs

Aliens In My Nest

Do I Have To Go To School Today?

Books in the Scooter Series by Larry Shles

Scooter's Tail of Terror

Larry Shles is a former science teacher of twenty three years who began writing and illustrating at the age of forty two. His first five books, which feature Squib the Owl, are autobiographical fables that chronicle his own search for self-esteem and acceptance.

More recently Larry, in response to an experience with substance abuse in his family, conceived a series of fables that explore the issues in addiction. SCOOTER'S TAIL OF TERROR, the first in this series, was created as part of his own recovery process.

Over the last several years, Larry has appeared in over twenty states and in Canada presenting programs in self-esteem, creativity, risk-taking and substance abuse to children and adults.

In addition to the numerous speeches and workshops on self-esteem that he has given to classroom teachers, teachers of the gifted, administrators, counselors, etc., he has recently begun to address educators more specifically in the areas of addiction.

Larry appears in as many as seventy five schools a year working with students, staff and parents in a celebration of uniqueness and self-worth. The day includes motivational assemblies and hands-on creativity workshops with students K-12, a one-half hour teacher inservice that stresses the vital role that teachers play in the lives of children and an evening parent meeting that emphasizes the parent's role in nurturing a child's spirit.

"I'll be real honest with you, we were not looking forward to sitting there for an hour listening to someone else tell us not to do drugs. We hear that all the time. But Larry really surprised everyone. He was a great influence on us today. We loved his work and his two characters, Squib and Scooter."

— 10th grader.

"I thought that the Scooter story was great! I feel like it reaches out and touches a lot of people."

— 8th grader.

Larry lives in St. Louis, Missouri with his family and is currently at work on future volumes featuring Scooter and Squib.

To schedule a visit by the author or for further information, write:

Larry Shles
P.O. Box 460451
St. Louis, MO 63146

Scooter was born with the most
remarkable tail anyone had ever seen.

"Scooter has been given a great gift," Mom whispered.

"Our son will go straight to the top!" Dad exclaimed. "With that tail, he is destined to become the greatest gymnast the forest has ever known."

Dad's dreams for his son soon came to pass. Scooter's tail was so quick to shift and adjust that it provided him with unerring balance. He could dive from the top branch of a tree and catch the lowest branch with one paw without ever crashing.

Unlike his father, Scooter wasn't convinced of his talent. "It's just luck," he thought. "One day I will miss."

He leaped from tree to tree with precision and grace. He scooted his way up meandering trunks in record time. And on flimsy branches where other squirrels slipped awkwardly and plummeted to the ground, Scooter remained upright and sure.

"It will never last," Scooter thought. "Someday I will fall short like all the rest."

Scooter's tail also had the remarkable ability to communicate the shifting moods of the forest. Squirrels came to him to learn from his tail. They watched as it quivered nervously to invisible danger or arched gracefully to the surrounding beauty.

"How can they believe my tail?" Scooter wondered. "There are times when even *I* don't trust what it says."

Scooter saw nothing unusual about his gifts. Even as he traversed the loftiest reaches of the forest, he found himself thinking about how far short he fell in the art of nest building or collecting nuts.

Often Scooter felt alone and different. He felt apart from the other squirrels.

Scooter's glorious tail shaded him from the heat of the sun. He stared out over the landscape and thought about his approaching adulthood. His future was out there — the place where he would have to live up to expectations — the place where he would have to fulfill his wonderful destiny.

And a thought nagged at him relentlessly . . . , "I could fail."

Scooter met Crystal. They exchanged glances and soft words. Soon they talked of the joys and promises of a life they could share.

Crystal nuzzled into his fur. "I will be there for you forever, Scooter," she whispered.

For a moment Scooter's doubts and questions melted away.

They built a leaf nest and began a family. They cached away nuts for the upcoming winter and began instructing their young on ways of surviving the harshness of nature.

Scooter, Crystal and their babies seemed to be the perfect family. Passersby would see them and their lofty nest. Secretly they longed for the successes and happiness they saw.

Scooter had the world by his tail . . . or so it seemed.

The vine appeared from nowhere. Scooter first noticed it as it inched its way upward toward his nest. It swayed with elegance and grace. He had never seen a vine like this. Each branch sported its own special kind of leaf and berry.

The subtly shifting motions, colors and aromas mesmerized Scooter. He watched the vine for weeks. His tail created poetry as it swayed gracefully, mirroring the incredible beauty of the leaves and tendrils.

The terror began on a beautiful Spring morning.
Scooter's old friend, Buzz, had stopped by.
"Hey, Scooter!" Buzz exclaimed. "Let's get high on your vine!"
Scooter looked at him in confusion.
Buzz broke into laughter.

"You don't know what to do with your vine, do you?" he chided. "I can't believe you've just been sitting around staring at it! The vine is peace and happiness, Scooter. All you have to do is snort it or smoke it or pop it or gulp it and excitement and pleasure will be yours!"

Then Buzz moved close. "Everybody's doing it," he whispered. "You have no idea what joys the vine will bring. The vine will be there forever for you. And once you use the vine, your tail will never fail you."

Other squirrels quickly found their way to Scooter's tree. They snorted, smoked, popped and guzzled the stuff of the vine. "C'mon Scooter, take a hit," Buzz urged. "We're all doing it."

Scooter gave in and drank some of the vine juice. He felt giddy, loose and numb. His worries and concerns melted away.

Quickly Scooter learned how to crumple drying leaves, light them and inhale the smoke. He learned how to crush the berries, mix the juice with fungus and gulp the mixture. He learned how to crush the seeds, blend them into pellets and pop them.

And the vine beckoned. "Come to me, Scooter. Devote yourself to me and I will be there forever to give you happiness."

Then the tendrils of the vine reached out and caressed him. He felt excited and frightened as he surrendered. The leaves wrapped themselves around him. His cares seemed to vanish within the reassuring cocoon.

Now he gave himself over to harvesting the vine. He spent little time with his family. He spent little time collecting nuts or repairing his nest.

Scooter became an expert at extracting juices, crushing leaves and grinding seeds.

He feasted, sometimes for days, on the pleasures of the vine. He was consumed with a longing for the feelings the vine gave him. It was becoming the center of his life.

As the months passed, Scooter spent even less time in his nest. He would sneak out in the middle of the night to smoke or pop or guzzle.

When morning came Crystal would plead, "Where have you been?"

And Scooter heard himself say, "I was out collecting nuts for the winter."

Scooter passed the winter in a corner of his nest amidst his cache of vine juices, leaves and seeds. He rarely spoke and when he did it was a barrage of foul language and accusations. Crystal and the babies were confused and frightened. They lived with a stranger.

"Look at what that vine is doing to you, Scooter," Crystal pleaded.

"NO! YOU ARE DOING THIS TO ME!" Scooter heard himself scream. "JUST GET OFF MY BACK!"

And he defiantly smoked and snorted and popped and guzzled in his family's face.

Spring came. Scooter was eager to see if his vine had survived. He lifted himself from the filth he had created and emerged from his nest.

It was then that he first caught sight of his tail. It had grown to resemble the vine. Behind his back his tail had transformed and taken on a life of its own. The vine that Scooter had been using had taken root in his tail.

And his tail turned to him and said, "I am your one true friend now, Scooter. Follow me."

"Where will we go?" Scooter asked.

"To fulfill our wonderful destiny," the tail replied.

"What is our destiny?" Scooter asked.

"You will find out soon enough," his tail replied. "But for now, take me back to the vine. I need more."

Soon Scooter lived next to the vine. He made no attempt to collect nuts. He forgot about his family.

The tail's gullet grew large as Scooter's eyes and ears clouded over.

Once again the tail spoke, "Take me back to the vine. I need more."

Feeling desperate, Scooter finally protested. "I don't feel well. I don't want more vine right now."

"TAKE ME BACK TO THE VINE, NOW!!" the tail screamed.

"I think I've had enough," Scooter whimpered. "Just look at me."

The tail laughed. Then it lunged toward the vine. Scooter was helpless as he was pulled along. The tail gorged.

"Actually, we don't need the vine," his tail whispered to him. "Tomorrow we will stop using it."

Tomorrow came and the tail laughed again and yanked Scooter back to the vine. "I WANT MORE!!"

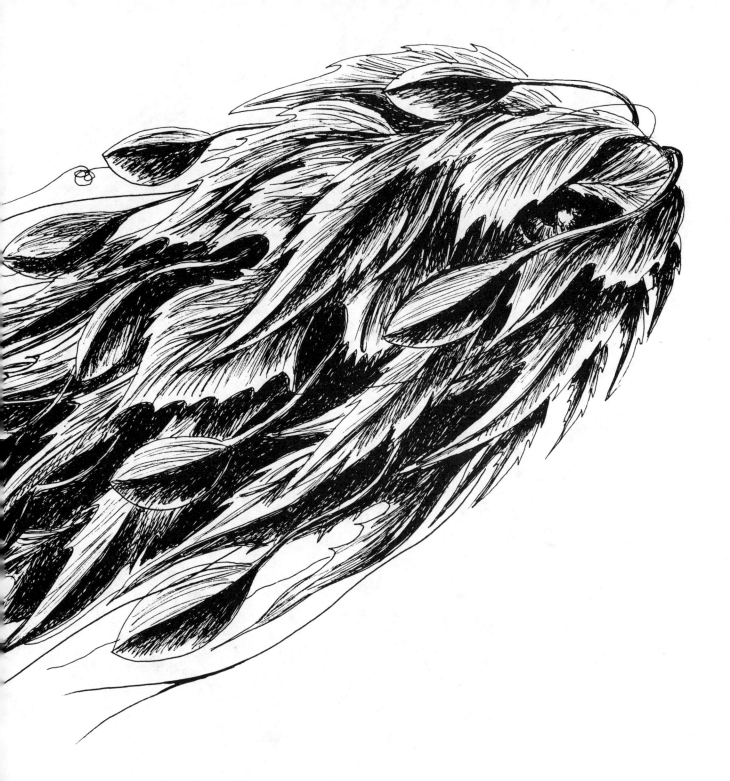

"I'm not really jerking you around," the tail said to Scooter. "You are really in control. You are simply choosing to scoot backwards for a while. Tomorrow you will be fine."

Tomorrow arrived and the tail again taunted Scooter.

"Let's go for a sprint through the trees," it said. "We will maneuver better than ever. Trust me."

Awkward and spastic, Scooter missed the first branch and came crashing to earth.

"That was great!" the tail exclaimed. "You are a better gymnast than ever!"

And Scooter believed.

"We must fulfill our destiny," the tail growled. "I WANT MORE VINE NOW!!!"

Each day the tail devoured more vine than it had the day before.

"I WANT MORE AND MORE AGAIN!!!" the tail bellowed.

Scooter was dragged through life, not seeing where he was going and too dazed to see where he had been.

"Our vine is becoming barren," the tail said. "Fertilize our vine. We must fulfill our destiny."

Scooter buried some decaying nuts at the base of his tree.

"Where are the nuts you have been collecting for the family?" Crystal asked.

"I was robbed on the way back to the nest," the tail said as it spoke through Scooter's mouth.

Crystal didn't know what to believe. "I don't understand what is wrong with you Scooter."

"There's nothing wrong with me, Crystal," the tail said, again speaking through Scooter's mouth. "YOU ARE THE ONE WITH THE PROBLEM!!"

Crystal felt crazy. Even when Scooter was away from the nest, the tail hung over the family like a frightening storm cloud.

No longer able to handle the fright, Crystal left with the babies. Scooter was alone. His nest crumbled from neglect. There were no nuts to get him through the winter. Scooter's senses dimmed even more.

"Look at what has become of our son," Mom said. "Where did we go wrong?"

"He had everything," said Dad. "Now look at him. It is shameful."

The terror reached its height on a beautiful Fall evening. Scooter's tail turned and faced him.

"It is time now," his tail said. "We are ready to fulfill our glorious destiny. We will become fertilizer for the vine."

The tail opened its jaws and swallowed what was left of Scooter.

He went hurtling to the ground.

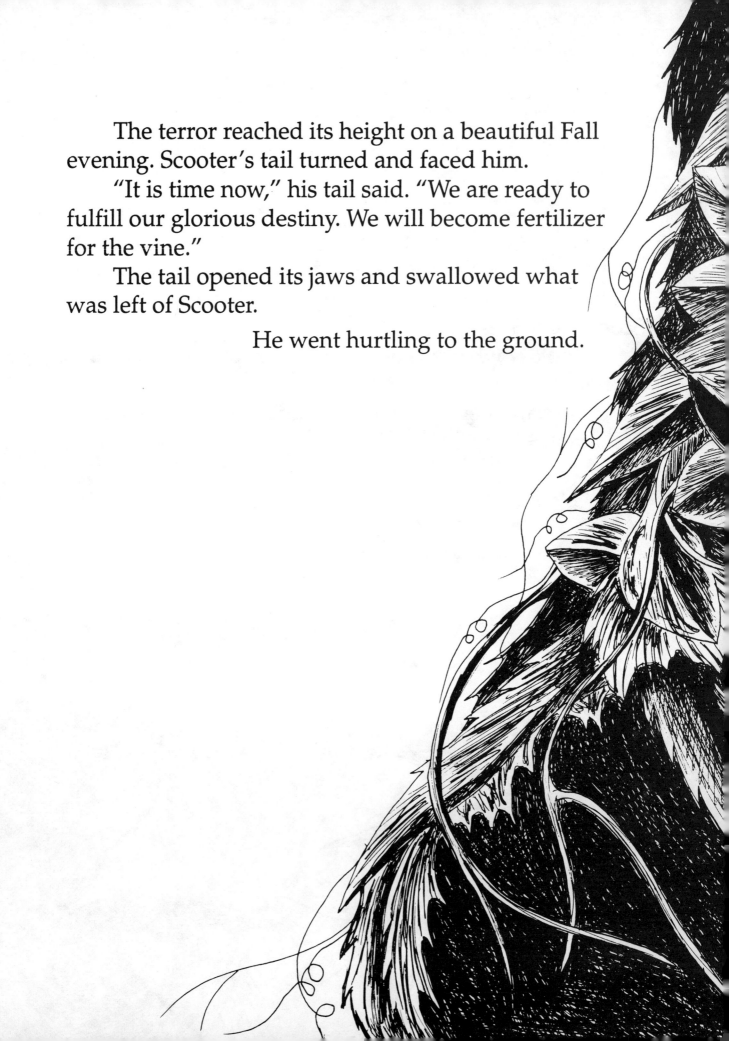

Barely alive and barely able to see through his clouded eyes, Scooter peered out from within the jaws of his tail. There he saw a vision of a squirrel that was gloriously whole and healthy.

The vision spoke.

"Man, Scooter. You are totally wasted!" It was Buzz.

"Perhaps you are ready now." Buzz continued. "Last winter I was as desperate as you are now. My tail was as horrible as yours. I rid myself of the terror. Follow me, Scooter, and you can become whole and healthy again."

Scooter couldn't imagine beginning anew.

"Where will we go?" he asked.

"You are going to climb to the top of your tree," Buzz said. "The vine will always be there to tempt you and the seeds of the vine will always be within you, ready to take root again. But I will be there next to you. Together we will overcome the power of the vine. When you reach the top you will be whole and with more wisdom than you can ever imagine."

Scooter looked up at his tree. He saw the immense leap he would have to make to reach the first branch. And he felt the weight of his monstrous tail. It seemed hopeless.

Then he felt Buzz standing next to him. Scooter
summoned up all his remaining strength and lurched
upward toward a destiny he could call his own.

To be continued . . . .

At Last . . . You Can Be That
"MOST MEMORABLE" PARENT/TEACHER/CARE-GIVER
To Every Person Whose Life You Touch Including Yours!

HELP KIDS TO: ❖ IMPROVE GRADES ❖ INCREASE CLASS PARTICIPATION ❖ BECOME MORE ATTENTIVE

ENCOURAGE & INSPIRE THEM AND YOU TO: ❖ TACKLE PROBLEMS ❖ ACHIEVE GOALS

AND

IMPROVE SELF-ESTEEM — BOTH THEIRS AND YOURS

Our authors are not just writers, but researchers and practitioners. Our books are not just written, but proven effective. All 100% tested, 100% practical, 100% effective. Look over our titles, choose the ones you want, and send your order today. You'll be glad you did. Just remember, our books are "SIMPLY THE BEST."   *Bradley L. Winch, Ph.D., JD — President and Publisher*

Sandy Mc Daniel &
Peggy Bielen

Project Self-Esteem, Expanded (Gr. K-8)

Innovative *parent involvement program.* Used by over 2000 schools/400,000 participants. Teaches children to respect themselves and others, make sound decisions, honor personal and family value systems, develop vocabulary, attitude, goals and behavior needed for *successful living,* practice *responsible behavior* and *avoid drug and alcohol use.*

0-915190-59-1, 112 pages, **JP-9059-1 $39.95**
8½ x 11, paperback, illus., reprod. act. sheets

Esteem Builders (Gr. K-8)

Teach self-esteem via curriculum content. Best K-8 program available. Uses 5 building blocks of self-esteem (security/selfhood/affiliation/mission/competence) as base. Over 250 grade level/curric. content cross-correlated activities. Also assess. tool, checklist of educator behaviors for modeling, 40 week lesson planner, ext. bibliography and more.

Paperback, 64 pages, **JP-9053-2 $39.95**
Spiral bound, **JP-9088-5 $44.95**, 8½ x 11, illus.

Michele Borba, Ph.D.

NOT JUST AUTHORS BUT RESEARCHERS AND PRACTITIONERS.

Naomi Drew, M.A.

Learning The Skills of Peacemaking: Communicating/Cooperation/Resolving Conflict (Gr. K-8)

Help kids say "No" to fighting. Establish WIN/WIN guidelines for conflicts in your classroom. *Over fifty lessons*: peace begins with me; integrating peacemaking into our lives; exploring our roots and inter-connectedness. Great for *self-esteem* and *cultural diversity* programs.

0-915190-46-X, 112 pages, **JP-9046-X $21.95**
8½ x 11, paperback, illus., reprod. act. sheets

6 Vital Ingredients of Self-Esteem: How To Develop Them In Your Students (Gr. K-12)

Put self-esteem to work for your students. Learn practical ways to help kids manage school, make decisions, accept consequences, make time, and discipline themselves to set worthwhile goals...and much more. Covers developmental stages from ages 2 to 18, with implications for self-esteem at each stage.

0-915190-72-9, 192 pages, **JP-9072-9 $19.95**
8½ x 11, paperback, biblio., appendices

Bettie B. Youngs, Ph.D.

NOT JUST WRITTEN BUT PROVEN EFFECTIVE.

You &
Self-Esteem:
The Key to Happiness
& Success

by Bettie B. Youngs, Ph. D

Bettie B. Youngs, Ph.D.

You & Self-Esteem: The Key To Happiness & Success (Gr. 5-12)

Comprehensive *workbook* for young people. Defines self-esteem and its importance in their lives; helps them identify why and how it adds or detracts from their vitality; shows them how to protect it from being shattered by others; outlines a plan of action to keep their self-esteem positive. Very useful.

0-915190-83-4, 128 pages, **JP-9083-4 $14.95**
8½ x 11, paperback, biblio., appendices

Partners for Change: Peer Helping Guide For Training and Prevention (Gr. K-12)

This comprehensive program guide provides an excellent *peer support program* for program coordinators, peer leaders, professionals, group homes, churches, social agencies, and schools. *Covers 12 areas,* including suicide, HIV / Aids, child abuse, teen pregnancy, substance abuse, low self esteem, dropouts, child abduction. etc.

Paperback, 464 pages, **JP-9069-9 $44.95**
Spiral bound, **JP-9087-7 $49.95**, 8½ x 11, illus.

V. Alex Kehayan, Ed.D.

100% TESTED — 100% PRACTICAL — 100% GUARANTEED.

V. Alex Kehayan, Ed.D.

Self-Awareness Growth Experiences (Gr. 7-12)

Over *593 strategies*/activities covering affective learning goals and objectives. To increase: self-awareness/self-esteem/social inter-action skills/problem-solving, decision-making skills/coping ability /ethical standards/independent functioning/creativity. Great *secondary resource.* Useful in counseling situations.

0-915190-61-3, 224 pages, **JP-9061-3 $16.95**
6 x 9, paperback, illus., 593 activities

Unlocking Doors to Self-Esteem (Gr. 7-12)

Contains *curriculum content objectives with underlying social objectives.* Teach both at the same time. Content objectives in English/Drama/Social Science/Career Education/Science/Physical Education/Social objectives in Developing Positive Self-Concepts/Examining Attitudes, Feelings and Actions/Fostering Positive Relationships.

0-915190-60-5, 224 pages, **JP-9060-5 $16.95**
6 x 9, paperback, illus., 100 lesson plans

C. Lynn Fox, Ph.D. &
Francine L. Weaver, M.A.

ORDER FROM: B.L. Winch & Associates/Jalmar Press, 45 Hitching Post Drive, Bldg. 2, Rolling Hills Estates, CA 90274-5169

CALL TOLL FREE — (800) 662-9662. • (310) 547-1240 • FAX (310) 547-1644 • Add 10% shipping; $3 minimum   4/92

PRACTICE prevention rather than intervention.
DEVELOPING positive self-esteem is our best weapon against drug and alcohol abuse.

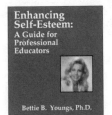

Good Morning Class— I Love You! Teaching from the Heart — ESTHER WRIGHT

Esther Wright, M.A.

Good Morning Class - I Love You (Staff)

Contains thought provoking quotes and ques-tions about teaching from the heart. Helps love become an integral part of the learning that goes on in every classroom. Great for new teachers and for experienced teachers who sometimes become frustrated by the system. Use this book to begin and end your day. Greet your students every day with: "Good morning class - I love you."

0-915190-58-3, 80 pages, **JP-9058-3 $7.95**
5¹/₂ x 8¹/₂, paperback, illus./**Button $1.50**

Enhancing Educator's Self-Esteem: It's Criterion #1 (K-12/Staff)

For the educator, a healthy self-esteem is job criteria No. 1! When high, it empowers us and adds to the vitality of our lives; when low it saps energy, erodes our confidence, lowers productivity and blocks our initiative to care about self and others. Follow the plan of action in this great resource to develop your self-esteem.

0-915190-79-6, 144 pages, **JP-9079-6 $16.95**
8¹/₂ x 11, paperback

Enhancing Self-Esteem: A Guide for Professional Educators — Bettie B. Youngs, Ph.D.

Bettie B. Youngs, Ph.D.

NOT JUST AUTHORS BUT RESEARCHERS AND PRACTITIONERS.

Elaine Young, M.A. with R. Frelow, Ph.D.

I Am a Blade of Grass (Staff)

Create a school where all — students, teachers, administrators, and parents — see themselves as both learners and leaders in partnership. Develop a new compact for learning that focuses on results, that promotes local initiative and that empowers people at all levels of the system. How to in this collaborative curriculum. Great for self-esteem.

0-915190-54-0, 176 pages, **JP-9054-0 $14.95**
6 x 9, paperback, illustrations

Stress Management for Educators: A Guide to Manage Our Response to Stress (Staff)

Answers these significant questions for educators: What is stress? What causes it? How do I cope with it? What can be done to manage stress to moderate its negative effects? Can stress be used to advantage? How can educators be stress-proofed to help them remain at peak performance? How do I keep going in spite of it?

0-915190-77-X, 112 pages, **JP-9077-X $12.95**
8¹/₂ x 11, paperback, illus., charts

STRESS MANAGEMENT FOR EDUCATORS A Guide To Manage Our Response To — Bettie B. Youngs, Ph.D.

Bettie B. Youngs, Ph.D.

NOT JUST WRITTEN BUT PROVEN EFFECTIVE.

"He Hit Me Back First!" SELF-ESTEEM THROUGH SELF-DISCIPLINE — EVA D. FUGITT

Eva D. Fugitt, M.A.

He Hit Me Back First: Self-Esteem Through Self-Discipline (Gr. K-8)

By whose authority does a child choose right from wrong? Here are activities directed toward developing within the child an awareness of his own inner authority and ability to choose (will power) and the resulting sense of responsibility, freedom and self-esteem. 29 seperate activities.

0-915190-64-8, 120 pages, **JP-9064-8 $12.95**
8¹/₂ x 11, paperback, appendix, biblio.

Self-Esteem: The "Affiliation" Building Block (Gr. K-6)

Making friends is easy with the activities in this thoroughly researched book. Students are paired, get to know about each other, produce a book about their new friend, and present it in class. Exciting activities help discover commonalities. Great *self-esteem booster*. Revised after 10 years of field testing. Over 18 activities.

0-915190-75-3, 192 pages, **JP-9075-3 $19.95**
8¹/₂ x 11, paperback, illustrations, activities

LEARNING THE SKILLS OF PEACEMAKING — Naomi Drew

C. Lynn Fox, Ph.D.

100% TESTED — 100% PRACTICAL — 100% GUARANTEED.

FEEL BETTER NOW 30 Ways to Handle Frustration in Three Minutes or Less

Chris Schriner, Rel.D.

Feel Better Now: 30 Ways to Handle Frustration in Three Minutes or Less (Staff/Personal)

Teaches people to handle stress *as it happens* rapidly and directly. This basic require-ment for emotional survival and physical health can be learned with the methods in this book. Find your own recipe for relief. Foreword: Ken Keyes, Jr. *"A mine of practical help"* — says Rev. Robert Schuller.

0-915190-66-4, 180 pages, **JP-9066-4 $9.95**
6 x 9, paperback, appendix, bibliography

Peace in 100 Languages: A One-Word Multilingual Dictionary (Staff Personal)

A candidate for the Guinness Book of World Records, it is the *largest/smallest dictionary ever published*. Envisioned, researched and developed by new Russian peace activists. Ancient, national, local and special languages covered. A portion of purchase price will be donated to joint U.S./Russian peace project.

0-915190-74-5, 48 pages, **JP-9074-5 $9.95**
5 x 10, glossy paperback, full color

ONE WORD MULTILINGUAL DICTIONARY — PEACE IN 100 LANGUAGES

By M. Kabattchenko,
V. Kochurov,
L. Koshanova,
E. Kononenko,
D. Kuznetsov,
A. Lapitsky,
V. Monakov.
L. Stoupin, and
A. Zagorsky

ORDER NOW FOR 10% DISCOUNT ON 3 OR MORE TITLES.

Joanne Haynes-Klassen

Learning to Live, Learning to Love (Staff/Personal)

Important things are often quite simple. But simple things are not necessarily easy. If you are finding that learning to live and learning to love are at times difficult, you are in good company. People everywhere are finding it a tough challenge. This simple book will help. *Shows how to separate "treasure" from "trash" in our lives.*

0-915190-38-9, 160 pages, **JP-9038-9 $7.95**
6 x 9, paperback, illustrations

Reading, Writing and Rage (Staff)

An autopsy of one profound *school failure*, disclosing the complex processes behind it and the *secret rage* that grew out of it. Developed from educational therapist's viewpoint. A must reading for anyone working with the *learning disabled, functional illiterates* or *juvenile delinquents*. Reads like fiction. Foreword by Bruce Jenner.

0-915190-42-7, 240 pages, **JP-9042-7 $16.95**
5¹/₂ x 8¹/₂, paperback, biblio., resources

Reading, Writing and RAGE

D. Ungerleider, M.A.

ORDER FROM: B.L. Winch & Associates/Jalmar Press, 45 Hitching Post Drive, Bldg. 2, Rolling Hills Estates, CA 90274-5169
CALL TOLL FREE — (800) 662-9662. • (310) 547-1240. • FAX (310) 547-1644 • Add 10% shipping; $3 minimum   4/92

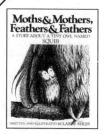

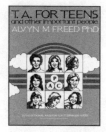